Ballet Bunnies

Joan Elizabeth Goodman

Marshall Cavendish Children

Special thanks to Kimm O'Connor, Shelley K. Grantham,
and Ingrid Thoonen-Rodriguez—three gifted teachers in the PeriChild
Program at Peridance Center, New York. Their expertise and inspiration
have been invaluable. Any missteps in *Ballet Bunnies* are mine, not theirs.
Turn-out positions have been modified for young bunnies to avoid injury.

Text and illustrations copyright © 2008 by Joan Elizabeth Goodman

All rights reserved
Marshall Cavendish Corporation, 99 White Plains Road, Tarrytown, NY 10591
www.marshallcavendish.us/kids

Library of Congress Cataloging-in-Publication Data
Goodman, Joan E.
Ballet bunnies: written and illustrated by Joan Elizabeth Goodman. — 1st ed.
p. cm.
ISBN 978-0-7614-5392-5
1. Ballet—Juvenile literature. I. Title.
GV1787.5.G66 2008
792.8—dc22
2007011907

The text of this book is set in Caslon 3 and Chalkboard.
The illustrations were rendered in acrylic paint.
Book design by Anahid Hamparian
Editor: Margery Cuyler

Printed in China
First edition
1 3 5 6 4 2

For Juliet Eve,
my grown-up
ballet bunny

Getting Dressed

Time for ballet class.
Brush ears, wash whiskers.

Pull on stretchy clothes, slip on slippers.

T-shirt

tights

ballet slippers

leotard

leotard

dance skirt

Come to the studio.

Come to dance!

Warm up bodies. Stretch and bend,
up and down, side to side. Keep tummies in.

Make pointy toes, flex feet.
Point and flex. Point and flex.

point flex

Reach up high. Stretch to the side. Touch your toes.

Ballet
Positions

Turn out

Parallel

Open book   Close book

Heels together, toes facing out.

Feet side by side,
toes facing front.

First Position—*Première*
Stand up tall, tummies in. Heels together, toes apart.

At the barre
Make a V with heels touching.

Free standing
Arms rounded in front, as if holding a big ball.

Second Position—*Seconde*

At the barre
Feet apart, making a wide V.

Free standing
Arms stretched out, slightly rounded.

Advanced Ballet Positions
(for bigger bunnies)

Third Position—*Troisiéme*

Front foot crosses
back foot at arch,
forming a T. Weight
is on both legs.

Fourth Position—*Quatrième*

Front foot moves
forward from third
position. Weight is
on both legs.

Fifth Position—*Cinquiéme*

Body is tall, feet
tightly crossed. Front
heel hugs back toe.

Port de Bras
(Arm positions)

First position arms
Rounded in front of the body
as if carrying a big ball.

Second position arms
Stretched out
from the shoulders.

Arms help the body turn.

Third position arms
One arm reaches
high over head,
the other stretches
to the side.

Fourth position arms
One arm reaches
high over head,
the other is rounded
in front of the body.

Fifth position arms
Rounded arms reach
high over head.

Jeté
Arms reach out.

Arms show feelings

Ballet
Exercises
at the Barre

Plié
Bending and stretching
the knees. Keep knees
in line with the feet
and back straight.

Demi-plié
Knees bend slightly,
heels stay on
the floor.

Demi-plié in first position   *Demi-plié* in second position

Grand plié
Deep knee bends, leaving a diamond space between knees. Heels up.

Relevé
Up on tiptoes.

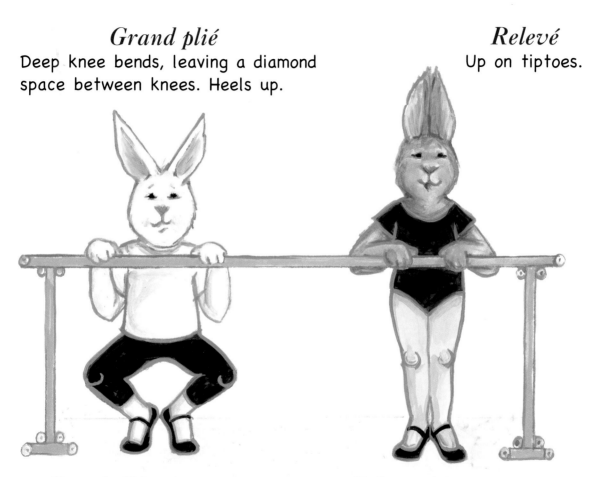

Grand plié in first position

Relevé in first position

Tendu
Pointing and stretching the feet.

Begin in first position.
Slide foot to side,
lift heel and point toe.

Slide foot back
to first position.

Now slide foot to front,
lifting the heel and
pointing the toe.

Return to first position.
Then work the other
foot, side and front.

Piqué
Tapping pointed toes, keeping legs straight.

Tap one pointy toe to the front.
Tap. Tap. Tap.

Tap it to the side.
Tap. Tap. Tap.

Tap the other pointy toe
to the front.

Tap it to the side.
Tap. Tap. Tap.

Passé
Touching toe to just
below the knee.

Arabesque
Standing tall on one leg, stretching
the other leg out behind.

Hop, skip, twirl, and wiggle!

twirl

Have fun!

wiggle

Sautés
Jumps! Heels touch floor on landing.

Face front.   Jump!   Face back.   Jump again. Face front.

Follow the leader.
Run on tiptoe.

Chassé
A gliding step. One foot chases the other.

Grand jetés
Big leaps!

Pretend to leap over a big puddle. Run, run, leap!

Révérence
A formal bow.

Curtsy or bow to thank the teacher and end the dance.

Glossary

Arabesque: Balancing on one leg, working leg extended behind, arms extended.

Barre: The dance studio bar to hold onto for balance.

Centerwork: Exercises and dance steps away from the barre.

Chassé: A gliding step. One foot chases the other.

Cinquiéme: Fifth position. Body is tall, feet tightly crossed. Front heel hugs back toe. Rounded arms reach over head.

Flex: Foot is flat

Jeté: Leap. (*Grand jeté:* Big leap!)

Leotard: Stretchy dancewear.

Parallel: Feet aligned, toes facing front.

Passé: Pointed toe touching knee of standing leg.

Piqué: Tapping pointed toes.

Plié: Knee bend. (*Demi-plié:* Small knee bend. *Grand plié:* Deep knee bend.)

Point: Stretched foot, pointed toes.

Port de bras: Arm positions.

Première: First position. Heels together, toes apart; feet form a V. Rounded arms held
    in front of body

Quatrième: Fourth position. Front foot slides forward from third position.
    Weight is on both legs. Rounded arm that matches back foot reaches high over
    head. Arm that matches front foot is rounded low in front of body.

Relevé: On tiptoe.

Révérence: A formal bow or curtsy.

Sauté: Jump

Seconde: Second position. Feet apart form a wide V. Arms stretched wide to each side.

Studio: A large open room with wooden floor, mirrors, and barre.

Tendu: Sliding the foot along the floor, pointing the toe and lifting the heel.

Troisiéme: Third position. Front foot crosses back foot at arch, forming a T.
    Weight is on legs. Rounded arm that matches back foot reaches high and
    slightly forward. Arm that matches front foot stretches to the side.

Turn out: Heels together, toes facing out.